ROXY'S
FRENCH DIARY

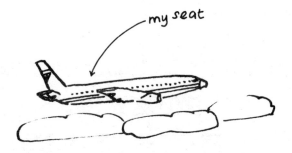

my seat

ORCHARD BOOKS
96 Leonard Street, London, EC2A 4RH
Orchard Books Australia
14 Mars Road, Lane Cove, NSW 2066
ISBN 1 85213 821 1 (hardback)
ISBN 1 85213 822 X (paperback)
First published in Great Britain 1995
First paperback publication 1996
© Branwen Thomas 1995
The right of Branwen Thomas to be identified as author and illustrator of this work has been
asserted by her in accordance with the Copyright, Designs and Patents Act, 1988.
A CIP catalogue record for this book is available from the British Library.
Printed in Great Britain

ROXY'S
FRENCH DIARY

Branwen Thomas

ORCHARD BOOKS

DO NOT READ

*Important message! All the French words in this book are in **bold** and are translated on the last pages!*

Monday

My name is Roxy. I've come to France on my own to stay with Granny because she asked me if I would like to. I thought it would be more fun than staying at home with my brother Nigel, who is a pest.

But we are all stuck on the plane because there is a big commotion at the airport—a very famous French film actress is waiting to meet her boyfriend and there are crowds of reporters and photographers and people trying to get her autograph.

Nigel

I am going to be an actress or else the first girl to win the Tour de France, which is a bike race. In the Tour de France you have to cycle up mountains, but I haven't tried that yet. I've brought my bicycle with me, although everyone said I couldn't. I have to keep practising.

I've never met this granny, who is my mummy's mummy, except once when I was zero and that doesn't count. She lives in France. Daddy says that she used to be an actress but no one has ever heard of her. Mummy says she still is an actress and a pain in the neck, like me.

People are getting off the plane at last, but I have to wait until someone comes to get me as I am an...

I have to wear a badge that has my name on it and everyone says, "Hello, Roxy. Travelling on your own?" So I give them my sickliest smile and so far I've made thirty francs.

Someone called Michelle has finally come to fetch me, so I must stop. I hope I get to see the actress.

This is France:

ENGLAND

THE TUNNEL

THE ENGLISH CHANNEL

BELGIUM

PARIS

SWITZERLA...

GE...

FRANCE

ATLANTIC OCEAN

THE ALPS

ITALY

WHERE GRANNY LIVES

GRANNY'S OTHER HOUSE
×

TOULOUSE

MEDITERRANEAN SEA

SPAIN

•••••••• = TOUR DE FRANCE ROUTE

Tuesday

Well, I did get to meet the actress. Michelle was quite beside herself and said, "Why did you not tell me Gabrielle Dupin is your granny?" And I said, "Why didn't anyone tell me?"

What happened was that I followed Michelle through passport control, and we found my bag and went through customs, and then we saw a woman dressed in a metallic-green leather motorbike outfit with matching cowboy boots, surrounded by crowds of people, and then, as soon as she

saw me standing by the 'Unaccompanied Children' collection point, she pushed her way through the reporters and flung her arms around me and kissed me and cried, "Roxy! **Chérie**! It is you, **n'est-ce pas**? I am Gabrielle." And then she whispered, "Your grandmother."

I told her she looked nothing like my other granny and asked what they call grannies in France. She went rather pale and quickly glanced at all the reporters standing around us.

"Gabrielle, **chérie**," she whispered. "Just call me Gabrielle."

Then she saw my bike.

"Oh, **chérie**! This is yours?" she asked, with a funny look on her face as though my bike smelt bad. Of course it's mine, I told her.

"Ah, well," she said, shrugging her shoulders. "We will do something about it."

the creepy one

My bike had to go in a taxi. Well, it had to because there wasn't room on Granny's motorbike. Yes, Granny had come to fetch me on her enormous metallic-green motorbike. Mum would have been really furious, but I'm not going to tell her. I will tell my pesky brother Nigel though, because he'll be jealous. Our other granny knits him jumpers with motorbikes on them. Nigel is her favourite.

So I whizzed into Toulouse on the back of Granny's motorbike. She had bought me a

helmet that matched hers and they had walkie-talkies in them so we could talk to each other. Or rather, so that Granny could talk to me. She told me about all the exciting things we were going to do. We went so quickly that soon we had left all the reporters behind. Maybe that is why Granny has the motorbike. I can't believe that Mum and Dad don't know she is so famous.

They don't speak to her much, though, because she and Daddy don't get on.

I was starting to get a tummy ache. Maybe it was because I ate too many biscuits and cakes and sweets on the plane.

Granny's apartment is right in the middle of town. We pulled up outside some huge wooden doors, which Granny opened with a secret number, then she took the bike into an amazing courtyard with a little fountain and heaps of flowers in pots. It is nothing like the block of flats where Aunty Cath lives.

Just then my bike arrived in the taxi, which was good because I was worried about it. I am saving up for a new one, but so far I've only got forty pounds—and thirty francs.

*"So, **chérie**," said Granny. (I have to tell you that **chérie** is the French word for darling and not what my other granny drinks, even though it sounds the same.) "I hope you are not too afraid of spiders."*

I don't much like spiders, but I wasn't going to tell her that. I followed her through another door that was a bit like a door in a castle and then up flight after flight of creaky wooden stairs and then down a very dark corridor where the light was broken (which was where the spiders were, but as I couldn't see them it was all right). Finally we found Granny's door. She must keep very fit. Her flat is at the very top and you can see the whole of Toulouse, nearly.

It was a relief to find a sofa and I was just about to sit on it when Granny said, "Now, Roxy, let us go and have tea."

I hadn't even seen my room and I don't like tea, but she was opening the door and telling me to come along, so I didn't have much choice. Off we went, back down all the dark corridors and creaky wooden stairs and out of the little castle door and through the big doors with the secret number into the street. Outside it was a lovely hot, sunny day and the streets were very busy. You could see that people knew who Granny was because they kept staring at her and taking photos. I pulled faces at them.

The place where we had our tea was really a cake shop. There were cake shops everywhere. I have never seen so many. It is a wonder that French people aren't all really enormous if they eat so many cakes, but they seem mostly to be small and thin. Perhaps they all live high up in wobbly apartment blocks like Granny.

I didn't really want a cake because of all the stuff I had eaten on the plane, but I thought I'd better have something. Granny thought I was being indecisive and said I could have two! I said, "No, thank you," in a polite voice that I use in times of emergency. There were some children at the next table drinking this really poisonous-looking green stuff, so I ordered it as well and it was mint squash! It was lovely, but it made my eclair taste really disgusting.

The wallpaper really was this horrible!

handle to stop you falling in!

BIG HOLE

CHASSE

I had to go to the toilet. They are called **les toilettes** in France. Granny pointed out the door, so I knew it was the right one. I went in but there wasn't a toilet. I looked everywhere, but there definitely wasn't one. What there was, though, was a sort of shower tray with two places to put your feet and a big hole in the middle. And a knob with **chasse** written on it. I pulled it and nothing happened, so then I pushed it. Suddenly there was

20

water everywhere and I had to jump back really quickly before my feet got wet. Well, I thought, that must be the toilet. The problem was, did I face forwards or backwards? I tried it both ways and decided it was probably much easier if you were a boy.

Granny told me in a loud voice afterwards that there weren't many toilets like that any more, except in bars and cafés and some restaurants. Most people had ordinary ones, and hers was an ordinary one too. I was glad.

It was about then that I suddenly noticed that most of the people eating cakes at the other tables were reporters. I knew because they all had notepads hidden behind their menus. Granny told me to ignore them.

"They are hoping I have a **rendezvous** with my boyfriend, Johnny Del Mondo, the film director, and they will not leave me alone. But do not worry, when I want to lose them it will be quite easy."

I pulled a face at them.

Then I had a thought. If Granny had a boyfriend who was a film director, maybe I could be in one of his films! That would be brilliant. Also I wondered if Mum and Dad knew Granny had a boyfriend. I decided I had better not tell them. They might be shocked.

"Am I going to meet him?" I asked.

"Yes, **chérie**. We shall go to my little house in the country on Friday and he will meet us there. But it is a secret." She gave me one of those looks they give in spy movies. I gave her one back.

As we left, everyone else seemed to leave as well. Granny said, "Let's have fun. We'll make their afternoon as miserable as possible."

She took me to a children's clothes shop

and soon the assistants were running around finding things for me to try on.

"**Alors!**" said Granny. "We will have this beautiful dress,

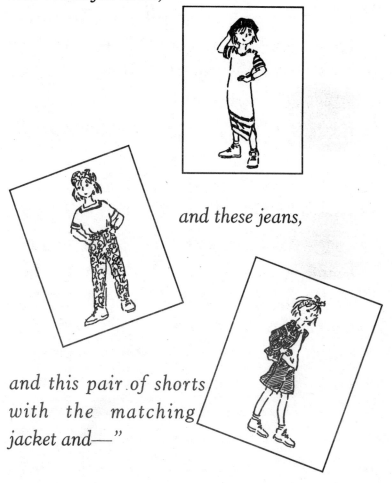

and these jeans,

and this pair of shorts with the matching jacket and—"

Granny's voice became a blur as I watched the reporters scribbling away behind the winter coats—"and we will buy that jacket for Nigel," she finished. They were finding it hard to keep up with her. I wouldn't like to have a job like that, but Granny says they get paid lots of money. I shall make lots of money when I am an actress. Granny says it is very hard to be an actress as there are so many people trying for so few parts. But I told her I would be all right as acting must run in the family. Mum is a maths teacher, though, so something must have gone wrong.

I can't remember all the other shops we visited and I don't suppose the reporters can either. At last we went home. My room was brilliant. I had a four-poster bed draped with mosquito nets and my very own television. The trouble was it was all in French. I did have a phrase book, but really they all spoke so quickly that it wasn't much help. *Granny shouted that she would teach me some useful phrases. . . and that I could take my bike with me when we went to her other house. I would need some time to practise for the Tour de France.*

Granny says everyone in France has big square pillows on their bed.

Granny's useful phrases:

Thank you = merci (mairsee)
Please = s'il vous plaît (seel voo play)
Hello = bonjour (bon-joor)
Goodbye = au revoir (oh revwah)

I can also say Je m'appelle Roxy (Jer mappelle Roxy), which means 'My name is Roxy'.

This one is difficult but I like it:

Qu'est-ce que c'est que ça? (kesker say kuh sa). It means 'What's that?' but the problem is I don't understand the answers!

Wednesday

Today Granny dragged me off to see the cathedral and the art gallery and the dungeon. We had lunch at a café and the reporters were there again. There was one particularly creepy one at the next table who I don't think had washed for at least a week. I think a reporter's life must be very boring. Of course, the day after tomorrow we will be meeting Johnny Del Mondo, but they don't know that.

*Granny took me to a very smart restaurant for supper. The **maître d'** (that's the head waiter) called me **mademoiselle** and told me I was to have the best seat at the* best table, which was right in the middle of the restaurant with little spotlights shining on it. I thought the window table looked better. Granny had the second-best seat. She said people fight each other to sit here.

The particularly creepy reporter was eating a sandwich in a café across the street. I could see him through the window.

When the waiter came to take our order, Granny said we would both have Eric's special. Eric was the chef. Granny said his special was always wonderful and that no one could come on holiday to France without having snails at least once. I thought I would throw up right there but, looking at the expensive carpet, decided it was not a good idea.

"You are not frightened to eat a few little snails surely?" said Granny. "Look, the children over there are eating them, and their parents have frog's legs."

Their legs looked quite normal to me, but then I realised Granny was talking about what they were eating.

The snails are not the same sort that we have in our garden at home, which Daddy gets rid of organically (he leaves them out for the birds to eat). When the waiter put the plate in front of me, I really felt sick but noticed the expensive carpet again. I

The one that got away.

dragged the snails out of their shells with the special fork and shut my eyes and put them in my mouth and... and they really didn't taste of anything much except garlic and tomatoes, and I like garlic and tomatoes, so I ate them all.

I was feeling very pleased with myself, and Granny was very pleased with me as well and let me have two puddings. Then Granny stood up and said she was just going to congratulate Eric, the chef. This must be something famous people do. But last year, when we were on holiday, Mum went and complained to the chef and it was very embarrassing, especially when she found all the supermarket ready-meal packets in the dustbin and demanded our money back. It was lucky for Eric that Granny liked her dinner.

As soon as she disappeared into the kitchen there was a funny clicking noise of cameras. I turned around to see who was taking photos, and when I turned back that pesky reporter was sitting in Granny's chair with his notebook out and started asking me questions—well, I suppose they were questions, but I didn't understand a single word, and his breath smelt strongly of all sorts of things I haven't tried yet and I don't want to try if I have to smell like that. I told him in English that I thought he ought to go and buy some mouthwash and would he please leave me alone, and that my name was Roxy Streep and that I was going to be starring in Johnny Del Mondo's next film. Then he mumbled **merci** something and picked up his notebook and shot out of the restaurant, just as Granny came back from thanking Eric for his snails. I didn't tell her what had happened.

French people sometimes eat and drink funny things. Here are some of the funniest:

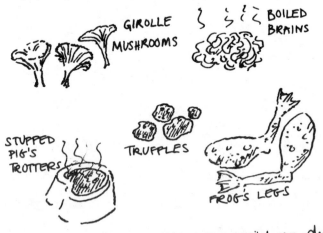

GIROLLE MUSHROOMS

BOILED BRAINS

STUFFED PIG'S TROTTERS

TRUFFLES

FROG'S LEGS

Granny says that all French children drink hot chocolate for breakfast. I think this is a good idea. And you're allowed to dunk your bread and jam into it.

Granny also says that French people like to eat tripe and brains and other things that I would rather not think about, so I won't mention them.

Thursday

This morning we went out to buy some **croissants** *for our breakfast and on the way to the* **boulangerie** *(that's a bread shop) we passed a* **maison de la presse** *with lots of people fighting to buy newspapers— obviously that was a newspaper shop.*

"What is this?" said Granny, snatching up a copy and pointing at my photo on the front page. "And how did they find out your name? And...Roxy...it says here you are to star in Johnny's new film—" she paused, looking up at the sky—"French Werewolf Three. *This is rubbish! Rubbish!"*

ROXY EST LA
NOUVELLE STAR DE
FRENCH WEREWOLF

I had never seen French Werewolf One *or* Two.

Granny didn't forget the **croissants** *but she was pretty mad. She stormed back to the apartment with me a few paces behind her.*

"How did they get the story?" she was mumbling. "How is it possible?"

I was wondering the same thing. The reporter must have understood everything I told him. I won't let him fool me again.

Granny telephoned the newspaper and I didn't need a phrase book to know what she was saying. She sounded just like Mum did when the washing-machine repair man didn't turn up. I'm glad we are going to the country tomorrow.

I've just found out that France doesn't have a king or queen. It has a president like the Americans. There used to be a king and queen, but in 1789 there was a revolution and they had their heads chopped off.

I've also found out that French children don't go to school on Wednesdays, but they go on Saturday mornings instead. I don't know if that is a good thing or a bad thing. But, horror of horrors, when you're eleven or twelve, you go to college and have to start at 8am! Then classes don't finish until 4.30pm! That's definitely a bad thing.

Friday

Granny's house has a swimming pool in the garden with a diving board. It was the first thing I saw. The house itself was all dark inside, until Granny went round opening the shutters. All French houses have shutters. There is a vine growing up the front of the house with grapes on it and there are fig trees and plum trees and apple trees, and there is an enormous barbecue that can roast a whole wild boar! Granny says that barbecued wild boar is wonderful if you are entertaining lots of people and that she once saw one run across the garden (before it got roasted).

Granny had to hire a taxi to bring my bike here, so I took it out and went exploring. There were a lot of people cycling. I decided to follow them, but we came to a very steep hill and they just all went up it so quickly that I got left behind. That's when I realised that I was lost. And when I also realised that I was being followed by a car full of reporters.

I stopped them and told them they must take me home. I told them that we were expecting Johnny Del Mondo very early the next morning and would they please leave me alone till then because I was very tired and of course it was quite true that I was to star in French Werewolf Three.

That fooled them.

They dropped me by the gates so Granny wouldn't see how I'd got back and then I went with Granny to relax by the pool. She was still muttering away under her breath about how awful the reporters were.

"I don't ever want to see another copy of that dreadful paper!" she said.

Just then there was a terrible noise as a helicopter popped up over the hillside and landed in the garden.

*"Ah, **chérie**, here is Johnny. I do hope he is not too upset by all this."*

A very happy-looking man wearing a

41

metallic-green flying suit climbed out of the helicopter. He had a huge smile on his face and he was waving a newspaper in one hand and holding a whole bundle of them in the other. The rotor blades were chopping through the air and bits of paper were flying all round the garden and apples were falling off the trees. One piece blew into the pool. It was the newspaper with my picture on the front page.

"**La publicité!**" I could hear him cry as he came running towards us. "**C'est merveilleux! C'est super!**" He was very excited.

Granny looked a little taken aback.

"Ah, Roxy," he said looking at me. "It is delightful to meet you. Come, we must go back to Paris immediately and finish filming. Of course, you must have a starring role, as one of the children who gets eaten by the werewolf."

I fell off the diving board.

Johnny Del Mondo didn't hang around. Within an hour we were all packed into the helicopter and my bike and Granny's bike

were locked in the garage. Granny's special supper for Johnny was shoved in the deep freeze and we were flying to the airport to catch the plane to Paris. I don't know about you, but I'd never been in a helicopter before and it was really exciting. We all had to wear earphones because the engine was so noisy and we could see all over the countryside because we were flying much lower than you do in an aeroplane.

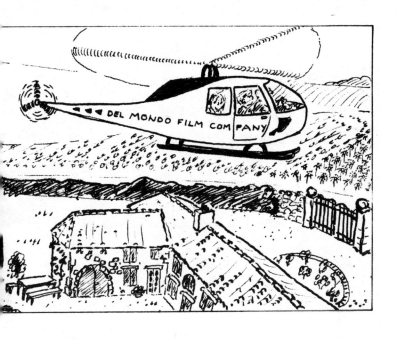

Then we flew to Paris, and I didn't need my passport because we were still in France and I did wonder if those horrid reporters had any idea of where we were going! They weren't on the plane.

That was because they were already in Paris. Johnny had told them before he had told us! Even the creepy one was there. Granny wasn't at all happy about this.

"You don't have to be eaten by a monster

in Johnny's silly film if it is not what you want. You can always say no."

But if I want to be an actress I have to start somewhere. And anyway, Johnny said he would pay me.

We went out for supper at La Coupole, which Granny says is a restaurant for famous people. I didn't recognise anyone but Granny knew everyone. She must have been kissed a hundred times at least. I have forgotten to mention that French people kiss each other all the time. They kiss each other when they say hello and they kiss each other when they say goodbye. You kiss right cheeks, then left cheeks and in Paris they like to kiss both cheeks again. Four times! Granny says it is all right to shake hands if you really don't want to kiss someone.

I shook lots of people's hands.

Tips on being famous:

Granny says you have to smile all the time, which means you have to clean your teeth really well. You have to smile even if you feel grumpy. This will be very hard if Nigel is being annoying, but Granny says you never know if someone is about to take your photo.

The other thing is that you must always look your best. You must remember to brush your hair and never look grotty or dirty.

It is also best to ignore photographers and reporters if it is possible, but you shouldn't be rude.

Being famous doesn't sound as much fun as I thought.

Roxy

Saturday

Today we had to get up really early. Granny says this is one of the bad parts about acting—you have to be in make-up by six o'clock!

We drove out to what looked like a big factory shed in the middle of the countryside next to a forest. It didn't seem very promising, but inside it was full of sets and lights and cameras and dressing rooms and canteens, and there were hundreds of people looking very busy. Johnny handed me over to someone called Letitia, who was going to make me up and do my hair. This is what I looked like when she had finished. The werewolf's dinner!

The werewolf was a gigantic hairy
monster with a man sitting inside it
operating a computer. It was really scary.
There were four other children and me and

we all had to run screaming "**Au secours!**" which sounds like "Oh seckoor" and is French for "Help".

Even though we all ran as fast as we could, the werewolf still caught us and ate us up. (I know I could have escaped if I'd been on my bicycle.)

It was very hot under all the camera lights. We had a couple of practise goes and then Johnny said "Shoot!" and the cameras started turning and the monster started chasing us and there were all sorts of people chasing the monster. It was really very easy. Until I discovered that we had to do the same thing twenty-six times—before lunch!

Granny looked a little anxious.

"What do you think about acting now, **chérie**?" she asked. "You discover it is hard work for the money, no?"

"The money!" I cried. "How much will I get?"

Do you know, I had completely forgotten that I would get paid. I will be able to buy my new bicycle now.

After lunch we all went outside to watch Johnny film the final scene. There were reporters and photographers everywhere. The cameras were all sitting on what looked like railway tracks so that they could follow the werewolf as he ran off into the woods and escape, so that there can be a French Werewolf Four.

Just behind his head a cameraman was hanging from a cable. I tried not to laugh. Johnny shouted at the reporters because they were getting in the way.

Laurent, the man who worked the monster, climbed inside, the cameras started rolling and Johnny shouted –"Shoot!" Everything was fine and the monster ran off towards the woods and Johnny shouted "Cut!"

But suddenly the werewolf went berserk. Laurent threw himself out and the monster just carried on without him, its legs flailing and its mouth opening and closing. It headed off right into the forest, where the reporters were hiding. They all screamed, but it just kept on snapping its jaws and chasing them. I think I saw it bite the really creepy one on his bottom.

Sunday

We all went back to Granny's house after the werewolf was found and the reporters had disappeared. Laurent has a broken arm and the monster is a write-off. But that won't stop there being a French Werewolf Four. Maybe I will have a bigger part next time.

We lounged around the pool and Johnny taught me how to dive off the diving board. He has given me enough money to buy the new bicycle I have been saving for. Now I can really get practising for the Tour de France.

Johnny went back to Paris after tea and we went back to Toulouse.

Granny said she'd had enough of Johnny and that she was going to find a new boyfriend. I told her she mustn't until after French Werewolf Four. I hope she will listen to me.

My Granny

Granny won't tell me how old she is but she told me she has been in twenty-three films, including a James Bond one. She's never won an Oscar, though.

She has been married twice. She says she got fed up with her husbands, but Daddy says they got fed up with her.

I think Granny is very glamorous. She has a whole room in her flat just for her clothes. Maybe when I am bigger she will give me some.

UN FILM DE JOHNNY DEL MONDO

·COMME VOUS VOULEZ·
avec
GABRIELLE DUPIN
HENRI PORTEJOIE
SYLVIE BLANC

Monday

This morning we went and had breakfast in a café and I had hot chocolate and a **pain au chocolate**, which is soft, flaky bread with melted chocolate in the middle. **Pain** is bread in French but it sounds like "pan".

We took a taxi to the airport because of my bicycle and all my new clothes. Granny had to buy me a new suitcase to put them in. I hope the clothes will still fit me as I have been eating so much.

At the airport Michelle was waiting with all sorts of things for Granny to sign, and when I told her that I was in Johnny Del

Mondo's new film, she asked me for my autograph, too. I shall have to practise my signature for when I am famous.

Granny helped me choose some perfume for Mum and **eau de toilette** for Dad. I will be very surprised if he likes it. I have got Nigel a radio with headphones to keep him quiet. I think I have been very generous.

I am not going to tell Mum and Dad about my holiday, because they might not let me come back. But I will tell Nigel, because he will be jealous.

My dictionary
of French words and phrases

alors! *(a-law) - so then!*

au secours *(oh seck-oor) - help! (useful when you're being chased by werewolves).*

boulangerie *(boo-lon-jer-ree) - a bakery*

c'est merveilleux *(say mer-vay-yer) - it's marvellous*

c'est super *(say soo-pear) - it's terrific*

chasse *(shas) - flush*

chérie *(sheri) - this means darling and my granny uses it all the time.*

croissant *(kwa-son) - a crescent-shaped, flaky bread roll*

eau de toilette *(oh de twa-let) - aftershave or perfume. (It actually means toilet water, but I won't tell my dad that!)*

gros bisous *(grow bee-soo) - big kisses*

les toilettes *(lay twalet) - this means toilet. An important one to learn!*

mademoiselle *(mad-em-mwa-zel) - this means Miss. They say* **madame** *if they are talking to your mum.*

maison de la presse *(may-zon de la press) - a newsagent*

maître d' *(may-tra dee) - the head waiter*

merci *(mair-see) - thank you*

n'est-çe pas? *(nez pas) - this just means isn't it?*

pain au chocolate *(pan oh shock-o-la) - the best thing to have for breakfast in France. It is flaky bread with chocolate in the middle. Deeeeelicious!*

la publicité *(la poo-bli-si-tay) - publicity (very important to a film director!)*

rendezvous *(ron-day-voo) - this is a word that is used in English but came from France. It means meeting.*

Tour de France *(Toor de Fronce) - this is the most famous bike race of all time, and I'm going to win it one day.*